OTTO

THE BOY WHO LOVED CARS

KARA LaREAU   SCOTT MAGOON

A NEAL PORTER BOOK ROARING BROOK PRESS NEW YORK

For SPB, car–o mio —K.L.

For Kara, who never steered me wrong —S.M.

Text copyright © 2011 by Kara LaReau

Illustrations copyright © 2011 by Scott Magoon

A Neal Porter Book

Published by Roaring Brook Press

Roaring Brook Press is a division of Holtzbrinck Publishing Holdings Limited Partnership

175 Fifth Avenue, New York, New York 10010

www.roaringbrookpress.com

Distributed in Canada by H. B. Fenn and Company Ltd.

Library of Congress Cataloging-in-Publication Data

LeReau, Kara.

Otto / Kara LeReau ; illustrated by Scott Magoon. — 1st ed.

p. cm.

"A Neal Porter Book."

Summary: Otto likes cars so much that he is interested in nothing else, until he wakes up one morning to find that he has become a car, unable to speak, eat, or play with his friends.

ISBN 978-1-59643-484-4

[1. Automobiles—Fiction.] I. Magoon, Scott, ill. II. Title.

PZ7.L55813Ott 2011

[E]—dc22

2010027186

Roaring Brook Press books are available for special promotions and premiums.

For details contact: Director of Special Markets, Holtzbrinck Publishers.

First Edition 2011

Book design by Scott Magoon

Printed in April 2011 in China by Macmillan Production Asia Ltd., Kwun Tong, Kowloon, Hong Kong (vendor code: 10)

1 3 5 7 9 8 6 4 2

There was once a boy named Otto.

He had a very smart, patient teacher and good friends.

Otto lived in a nice house with his mother, who loved him very much.

But above all places

and things

(and even most people),

Otto loved cars.

Each morning, Otto would wake up and eat his favorite cereal.

He'd play with his cars all the way to school—
and when he got there, he couldn't wait for recess,
where he would insist on playing Race Around the
Playground with his friends, Chevy, Mini, and Kia.

One night, after playing with cars, and drawing some cars, and reading about cars, Otto put on his pajamas and got into bed.

His mother came to tuck him in.

"Time for a new story?" she asked.

"I don't want to hear it unless it's about cars," said Otto.

His mother sighed.

"Ah, well, my little speedster," she said, kissing the top of his head, "you don't know what you're missing."

Then she turned out the light and closed the door—leaving Otto to count Jeeps until he fell asleep.

The next morning, when Otto woke up, he just didn't feel like himself.

And with good reason.

Because somehow, overnight,

Otto had become a car.

Unfortunately for Otto, no one else seemed to notice the difference.

When he opened his mouth to say, "Pass the Wheelies"

at the breakfast table, he made a noise

that sounded like this:

Honk-honk, HONK!

"This is a kitchen, not a garage," Otto's mother said.

So Otto didn't get to eat his favorite cereal.

And he couldn't fit on the school bus, so, of course, he had
to drive himself to school.

And traffic was terrible that morning, so Otto was very late . . .

which made Mrs. Dodge, his teacher, very angry.

Otto tried to explain, but instead he sounded like this:

Honk! Honk-honk, Honk-honk-honk!

So he was not only very late, but very LOUD, which made Mrs. Dodge even angrier.

Otto spent his morning parked in the Time-Out Corner.

Otto had forgotten his lunch (and couldn't have eaten it anyway, since a car can't eat), so he idled by the window and looked forward to recess, his favorite part of the day.

Finally, Mrs. Dodge took the class out to the playground.

"Let's play!" Otto shouted to Chevy and Mini and Kia,

but it sounded like this:

Vroom-vroom! VROOM!

"Geez, Otto," Chevy said. "You want to play

Race Around the Playground again?"

"That's all he ever wants to do," said Mini.

"Let's swing on the monkey bars!" said Kia.

And they all did. Except for Otto.

Because, of course, cars can't swing on monkey bars,

or anything else for that matter.

So Otto raced around, and around, and around . . .

all by himself.

After school, it took Otto forever to get home (traffic again),

and when he finally did he was miserable.

He knew he couldn't eat whatever his mother made for dinner,
so he went to bed very, very, very hungry.

He didn't play or draw or read, because
cars can't do any of those things.

So Otto started to cry.

Of course, it didn't sound like crying.

It sounded like this:

Sputtery-sputtery-sput!

Clunkity-clunky-clink!

Clankety-sputtery-clank!

Sputtery-spittery-clunk!

Sputtery-clink!

Sputtery-clank!

Sputtery-clunk, clunk,

Clink!

Which is what cars sound like
when they are broken-down
or running out of gas,
and Otto was both.

His mother couldn't help overhearing the noise.

"What's the matter?" she said. "You haven't been yourself all day."

"I'm sick of cars," Otto honked softly into his pillow. "I just want to be a boy again."

"You've been living and breathing one thing for too long," she said. "Everyone has to switch gears sometime."

Then she kissed his hood and turned out the light.

"Sleep tight," she said, closing the door, "and don't let the spark plugs bite."

Otto laid awake for a long time, sniffling and sputtering and thinking about what his mother said, until, finally, he ran out of gas and went to sleep.

The next morning, when Otto woke up, he wasn't a car. Instead, somehow, he was himself again. And he made sure to enjoy the difference.

When he got to the breakfast table, Otto's mother started to pour his bowl of Wheelies.

"Thank you," said Otto, kissing her on the cheek. "But I think I'll have an English muffin, please."

When he got to school (on time), Otto was on his very best behavior, much to Mrs. Dodge's delight.

At lunch, he savored every bite of his peanut-butter-and-jelly sandwich.

And of course, Otto couldn't wait for recess, to see Chevy and Mini and Kia and play some of their games, like Monkey Bar Swing-a-Long, and Simon Says, and Tag (which was a lot like racing, with just a few more rules, Otto thought).

That night, when his mother came to tuck him in, Otto was already in his bed,

waiting patiently.

"I think it's time to switch gears," said Otto.

"It is?" said his mother.

"Yes," replied Otto. "I'm ready for a new story. And not one about cars."

"Really?" said his mother.

"Well," said Otto, "it's about *one* car who turns into a boy. And I'm

going to tell it to you."

"I'm listening," said his mother.

So Otto began.